PETE'S PLACE

Coffee to Go

NOX PRESS

books for that extra kick to give you more power
www.NoxPress.com

Also by Elise Leonard:

The **JUNKYARD DAN** series: (*Nox Press*)

1. Start of a New Dan
2. Dried Blood
3. Stolen?
4. Gun in the Back
5. Plans
6. Money for Nothing
7. Stuffed Animal
8. Poison, Anyone?
9. A Picture Tells a Thousand Dollars
10. Wrapped Up
11. Finished
12. Bloody Knife
13. Taking Names and Kicking Assets
14. Mercy

THE SMITH BROTHERS (a series): (*Nox Press*)

1. All for One
2. When in Rome
3. Get a Clue
4. The Hard Way
5. Master Plan

A LEEG OF HIS OWN (a series): (*Nox Press*)

1. Croaking Bullfrogs, Hidden Robbers
2. 20,000 LEEGS Under the C
3. Failure to Lunch
4. Hamlette

The **AL'S WORLD** series: (*Simon & Schuster*)

Book 1: Monday Morning Blitz
Book 2: Killer Lunch Lady
Book 3: Scared Stiff
Book 4: Monkey Business

The **LEADER** series: (*Nox Press*)

★ Honor
★ Courage
★ Respect
★ Service
★ Integrity
★ Commitment
★ Loyalty
★ Duty

PETE'S PLACE (a series): (*Nox Press*)

1. On Ice
2. Coffee to Go

PETE'S PLACE

Coffee to Go

Elise Leonard

NOX PRESS
books for that extra kick to give you more power
www.NoxPress.com

Leonard, Elise
PETE'S PLACE (a series) / Coffee to Go
ISBN: 978-1-935366-33-1

Copyright © 2010 by Elise Leonard.
All rights reserved, including the right of reproduction in whole or in part in any form. Published by Nox Press.
www.NoxPress.com

First Nox Press printing: September 2010

books for that extra kick to give you more power

This book is dedicated to Felton Scott,
(AKA: "Scott") in Casper, Wyoming.
You are the *exact* image I have in my mind
of Pete (the main character in this series).
When I saw your picture,
I almost fell out of my chair with shock!
You have Pete's strength, his stature,
his good looks, his inner dignity and,
hopefully, his sense of humor. ☺
In my mind, you *are* Pete.

This book is also dedicated to Valeri Geyko in
New Mexico, whose first language is Russian.

English is a *very* difficult language to learn!
I was *so* happy to hear that you enjoy
reading my books. ☺

I'd like to thank
Muncie Hansen, Program Coordinator,
and Will Steinsiek, Executive Director
of ReadWest for
providing my books for their learners.
You've got a great program there,
and I think everyone knows how much I love
New Mexico. Keep up the great work!

~Elise

Chapter 1

My phone rang.

"So what have you been up to?" my handler asked.

"Trying to heal up."

"Have you been staying out of trouble?" she asked.

I thought of Max.

And his funeral home break-in.

And the theft of his mother's body.

And the four-hour window where we had

to keep the body cold.

It was a good thing that she could not see my grin.

"Of course I've been staying out of trouble," I replied.

She laughed.

"Why do I doubt that?" she asked.

"I don't know," I said. "It's not at *all* like me to get into trouble."

Again, she laughed.

"So what *have* you been up to?" she asked.

I thought about that.

Let's see. I went to Max's mom's funeral.

I felt I owed it to him.

I mean, I helped him with the heist.

Then I helped him get his mom to Pleasant Meadows.

They were a little shocked at the way their latest client was delivered.

Coffee to Go

The nice lady was a bit thrown off.

She sputtered when we walked in with Max's mom.

"This is not the usual way we receive..."

She had no idea how to finish that sentence.

But I understood.

I'm sure it wasn't every day they got a dead body delivered the way we brought the body in.

I had to chuckle as I recalled the scene.

We walked in as the place opened.

We were carrying a body wrapped in a wool blanket.

We'd kept her on ice, so she was pretty cold.

Then Max said, "Where do you want her?"

I thought the woman would swallow her tongue.

Chapter 2

But she got over it.

She composed herself pretty quickly.

I was impressed.

"You can bring her to the back," the nice lady said.

"Thank you," Max said.

The guys in the back were a bit shocked, too.

But then they were happy, when they saw that we'd kept her on ice.

Coffee to Go

"Don't worry," they'd said. "We'll take good care of her."

And they did.

The funeral was nice. (As funerals went.)

I don't think any funeral is actually *nice*.

I mean, it's a funeral.

How nice can it be?!

But they'd handled everything with dignity.

A lot more dignity than how Max's mom had come *in* to Pleasant Meadows.

"So how are you feeling?" my handler asked.

"My ribs are still sore."

"Put ice on them," she said.

I had to smile.

"Could you be ready for a job soon?" she asked.

"That depends," I said.

"On what?" she asked.

"What kind of job is it?"

"You'll like this one," she said.

"Oh yes?" I asked "Why?"

"It's close to home."

In my old age I was getting a bit grumpy about all the travel.

Every mission I went on was far away.

Really far away.

You would not *believe* the places I'd been.

I seem to travel all over the world.

In the last year I'd been to Iran, Iraq, Egypt, Yemen and Abu Dhabi.

I'd been to Syria, Lebanon, Israel, Turkey and a bunch of what I call the "istans."

You know... Pakistan, Afghanistan, Turkmenistan, and a bunch of other "istans."

I was in Libya, Ghana and Zambia.

I'd been to Brazil, Peru, Chile, Columbia and Venezuela.

I was in China and Japan, and many points in between.

Coffee to Go

I'd been to Russia, Serbia, Greece, Spain, Norway and England.

I'd been to places where I couldn't even pronounce their names.

And that was just this past year.

I hope the agency was getting frequent flyer miles for me.

Because they sure were adding up.

With the number of miles I fly? *Someone* could be getting a free trip to Tahiti each month.

Ahhh. Tahiti. That might be nice.

Better than the war-torn or troubled places where I *usually* ended up.

But even Tahiti wasn't close to home.

"So what do you consider to be close to home?" I asked my handler.

As far as she was concerned, South America was "close to home."

Chapter 3

"The job's in Vermont."

That made me crack up.

"*Vermont*?!" I sputtered.

My mind was racing.

What could possibly be going on in Vermont that could demand my presence?!

"Are the maple trees refusing to supply syrup?" I asked.

I laughed out loud.

"Are they forming a cell, and fighting for

their rights?" I asked.

My laughter was hearty.

"Have they gone *rogue*?" I asked between bouts of laughter.

My handler waited for me to finish.

After about five minutes she spoke.

"Are you done yet?" she asked.

"Wait," I said. "I think I have one more."

"Why don't you keep it to yourself?" she offered.

I had to smile.

"You're joking about Vermont, right?" I asked.

"No," she said.

"Vermont?"

"Right."

"Is there a Vermont in Iraq I don't know about?"

She laughed.

"No."

"Is there a Vermont in Korea I've never

heard of?" I asked.

"Not to my knowledge," she replied.

"Is there a Vermont in Africa?" I asked.

"Not that I'm aware of," she said. "And if there *is*, that's not the Vermont we are sending you to."

This had to be a trick.

"So which Vermont are you sending me to?" I asked.

"Vermont, Pete. Just... Vermont."

"As in... the state? In America?" I asked.

"Yes."

Chapter 4

"That's so nice of you guys. Thanks," I said.

They were sending me to recoup in Vermont.

That was nice.

"I *would* prefer Tahiti, though," I said.

"I'm sure you would," she said. "But that's not where a major arms deal is going down."

"A major arms deal?" I asked.

"That's what I said."

"In *Vermont*?!" I asked.

"That's what we're hearing."

"Why Vermont?" I asked.

"Who knows?!" my handler replied.

"That seems so weird to me."

"To us, as well," she said. "But we can't take a chance."

"Are you sure you're not messing with me?"

She snorted a laugh.

"I wish I was," she said.

"There's *really* a major arms deal going down in Vermont?"

"That's what we heard," she said with a sigh.

"These guys sure are getting bold," I said.

"You can say that again."

"Where are they coming from?" I asked.

"All sorts of places."

Coffee to Go

"So it's not a two person deal?"

"No," she said. "It's more like an auction."

"How many will be there to bid on these weapons?"

"We don't know," she said.

"And that's why you want *me* there."

"Right."

"How am I doing this?" I asked.

"You can do it any way you'd like."

"Am I bidding? What's my cover?"

"We're leaving that up to you," she said.

Chapter 5

I thought about my new job.

Why can't these terrorists do things like everyone else?!

Can't they post their weapons on eBay?

It would make *my* job a lot easier.

You can buy *anything* on eBay!

A potato that looked like Elvis sold for eleven thousand dollars.

A potato *chip* that looked like Abe Lincoln sold for five thousand dollars.

Coffee to Go

I bet the seller for the chip was happy!

I mean, it was for a *slice* of a potato.

Not even the whole potato, like Elvis!

I wondered if he could get a few potato chips that looked like Abe Lincoln.

I mean, if it were on *one* slice, it *must* have been on more.

Let's see.

What if he had five slices that looked the same.

At five thousand dollars a slice.

Wow.

That would be twenty-five thousand dollars!

For five slices of potato.

Five potato chips.

People never cease to amaze me.

There were many other weird things sold on eBay, too.

Strange stuff is *always* posted there.

And people flocked to pay a lot of money

for them.

I love seeing the bids for ghosts.

Who in their right mind bids on eBay for ghosts?!

One guy tried to sell his liver.

Another guy tried to sell his kidney.

Of course those auctions were stopped. It's illegal to sell body parts.

But how do you know what you're even *getting*?!

The liver could come from an alcoholic.

And the kidney? That could come from someone who has to go to the bathroom every five minutes!

You just don't know what you're *getting* on eBay.

Chapter 6

Some lady sold the name of her fourth child on eBay.

What happened? Did she run out of names?!

She came up with three.

It was too tiring to come up with a fourth name?

If Octo-Mom had done that? She would have made a *fortune*.

There was only one problem. You end up

with really weird names.

Like that lady.

Her fourth child is named "Golden Palace."

It's said that some casino won the auction.

I heard that they paid fifteen thousand five hundred dollars for it.

I'll bet *that* kid's going to love his mother when he becomes a teen.

And by that time? I'll bet the money will be long spent.

I'm sure it wasn't put away for the kid's college fund.

And speaking of casinos. I heard a casino bought a grilled cheese sandwich.

They paid twenty eight *thousand* dollars for it.

It wasn't even a whole sandwich!

It had the face of the Virgin Mary on it.

(The sandwich. Not the casino.)

Coffee to Go

Now let's get things straight.

I saw a picture of the sandwich.

Maybe there was an image of a lady grilled onto it. Maybe there wasn't.

It was kind of blurry.

But even if there *was* an image of a lady on it. How does anyone know it was the image of the Virgin Mary?

How do we know it wasn't an image of some lady who sells fish somewhere?!

But twenty eight *thousand* dollars?

For part of a grilled cheese sandwich?

That's just nuts.

Then some people found a Dorito chip in their bag.

They thought it looked like the Pope's hat.

You know the one.

That really tall pointy hat.

So they took a picture of it and put it on eBay.

And get this. It's said that the same casino bought that chip.

They paid twelve hundred for it.

That's right.

One thousand two hundred dollars.

For one Dorito chip.

A Dorito chip that looked like the Pope's hat.

But still.

One... Dorito... chip.

Casino's have *way* too much money!

But you've got to think about it.

Where do they *get* all that money?!

You've *got* to know the answer to that.

They keep taking it from us hard-working folks.

When will we learn?!

The house *always* wins!

And what do they do with that money?

They buy a grilled cheese sandwich. And a single Dorito chip.

Coffee to Go

Just those two items set them back almost thirty thousand dollars!

Is that nuts or what?!

Somebody sold the "meaning of life" on eBay.

That went for three dollars and twenty six cents.

Not three dollars even.

Not three fifty.

But three dollars and twenty six cents.

I've got to say, we've got our priorities all messed up!

How come the meaning of life sold for less than three fifty?!

The meaning of life should at *least* be worth a couple thousand.

Chapter 7

"Pete? Are you there?" my handler asked.

"Yes. Sorry. I was thinking about eBay."

She laughed.

"Sorry to disturb you," she said.

"It's okay," I cracked. "But it makes me wonder."

"About what?" she asked.

"Why can't these guy sell their weapons on eBay?!"

"Excuse me?" she asked.

"You can buy *anything* on eBay!"

She laughed again.

"That's coming soon, I'm sure," she said.

"Well, you *would* need good Internet access," I said.

"You'd think," she said.

"Probably can't get that in caves," I noted.

"Most likely not," she said.

"So these creeps have to come out of hiding anyway," I said.

"They'd have to," she said. "To buy their weapons."

"And they might as well go to Vermont," I said.

"Might as well," she repeated.

"So I guess I'll go there too," I said.

"Might as well join the party."

I smiled.

I'll have to decide.

Should I go as a buyer?

Or should I go as just a guest?

Maybe I should just pretend I'm a local.

I had to think about it.

"When is this party going down?" I asked.

"In six days."

"That doesn't give me much time to plan," I said.

"We just found out."

"Okay," I said.

"I'll call you in 48 hours," she said.

"I'll let you know what I'll need then," I said.

"Roger that," she said.

Chapter 8

I could go as a buyer.

But that would make the seller nervous.

He'd never seen me before. So he might get spooked.

Of course he'd run a background check.

But the agency would handle that.

So that wasn't a problem.

The problem was getting in the door.

The seller might only want to deal with known slime-bags.

And I didn't have enough time to *become* a known slime-bag.

If I'd had a couple of months? I could have won the "slime-bag of the year" award.

Hands down!

I would have fit right in with these guys.

They would have been coming to *me* for ideas on how to be a better slime-bag.

But I didn't have that kind of time.

I didn't have months.

I only had days.

You can't build street cred in days.

Good street cred took time.

So I had to think of something else.

I *could* go as a guest of the bed and breakfast.

But that could be a problem.

The arms seller might have rented the whole inn.

This way his buyers were protected.

Sort of a "slime-bags only" weekend at

the inn.

That way everyone is protected.

You know how they have "ladies night" at certain spots?

Well, this would be "arms dealer days" at the inn.

The only thing was that you couldn't tell by looking at them.

It was easy to tell who got in on "ladies night."

Not so easy to tell who got in on "arms dealer day."

They didn't carry around arms dealer ID cards, either.

Chapter 9

Arms dealers don't all look alike.

Many *do* like to use hair gel.

Or at least *some* kind of hair care product.

But for the most part, they all look different.

So for that reason, I could fit in.

A big black man could fit in a lot of places.

But I did have a problem once, in

Coffee to Go

Norway.

I had the accent down.

It was perfect, really.

But they just didn't buy it, for some reason.

Anyhow. The "going as a guest" thing was probably not a good idea.

In case the inn was closed to the public.

I had to come up with something else.

But what?

I went outside to load up the truck.

I did what I always do.

I took out the ice.

I put the ice in the bins.

I put the cans of soda in the ice.

I put the sandwiches on top.

I put the chips on the left side.

I put the sweet snacks on the right side.

You know, the cookies, cakes and candy. Stuff like that.

I went through my check list.

Elise Leonard

I turned on the oven.
I threw a few slices of pizza in there.
I was ready to do my route.
And then it hit me.

Chapter 10

I checked my watch.

I knew she would call in four minutes.

Two days ago she said she'd call in 48 hours.

In four minutes, it would be 48 hours.

To the second.

If my handler was anything? She was on time.

Always.

You could set your watch to her.

I walked to the back of the truck.

I plucked out a bag of chips.

I had four minutes to wait.

So I ate the chips.

But first I looked at each chip.

Just in case.

Hey, some of them could be worth thousands.

The phone rang. Right on time.

"So what are you doing?" she asked.

"Looking at potato chips."

"Why?" she asked.

"To see if they look like Abe Lincoln."

"What if they do?" she asked.

"I make a fortune on eBay."

She laughed.

"You're really into that whole eBay thing," she said.

"Just keeping my options open."

She laughed again.

"So what if they don't?" she asked.

Coffee to Go

"Don't what?" I asked her.

"Don't look like Abe Lincoln," she said.

"I eat them."

She laughed.

"Sounds like you're really busy," she said.

"I've been busier."

"Did you decide how you want to do this job?" she asked.

"Yes I did," I said.

"What do you need?" she asked.

"Any chance you can get me a C-130?"

Chapter 11

She paused for a moment.

"I can get you anything you ask for," she said.

I grinned.

"*That's* why I like you so much," I said.

"Because I give you stuff?"

"Yeah."

"I feel so used," she said.

"Hey," I said. "If *I* could give *you* a military transport aircraft, I would."

Coffee to Go

"Thanks," she said. "I feel the love."

She cracked me up.

"So when do you need it?" she asked.

"When can you get it to me?"

"Ten minutes," she said.

"Take your time," I said. "I need to finish my route."

"Are you still doing that?" she asked.

"I *love* my lunch truck!"

"So you keep saying," she said.

"What's not to love?" I asked.

"Our nation's top agent doesn't need to be doing it."

"I know I don't *need* to do it," I said. "Hey, wait a minute. Did you say I was the *top* agent?"

"That's what I said."

"What happened to the new pup?" I asked.

There was this new guy.

He was an amazing agent.

Young. Talented.

Shifty as can be!

And smart as a whip.

"He's gone," she said.

"Gone as in out of town?" I asked.

"Gone as in gone."

"Kicked out of the agency?" I asked.

"Dead, Pete. The kid's dead."

I had to stop and soak that up.

It reminded me that we played with a very tough crowd.

I tried not to think about that.

But at times like this?

I thought about it.

"I'm sorry," I said softly.

"Yes," my handler said. "Me too. He was a good agent."

Chapter 12

"When do you need the C-130?" she asked.

"Can you get it to me in about 4 hours?" I asked.

"Sure. Where do you want it?"

"Have them land at the private airstrip down the road from my house."

"Okay, Pete," she said.

I knew she was writing that down.

"Do you need anything else?" she asked.

"No, that's it."

"You don't need a car?" she asked.

"Nope. Thanks."

"We've got a nice Ferrari Enzo."

"What color?" I asked.

"Red."

"Sounds nice. But no thanks."

"Want a Lamborghini?" she asked.

"Nah," I said. "Not this time."

"You might need some cool toys," she mentioned. "If you're going to play with these guys."

"I know," I said. "I've got it covered."

"So what are you transporting?" she asked.

"My, ah..."

I knew this was going to freak her out.

So it was hard to tell her.

I knew that losing that young agent was hard.

It was hard for all of us.

Coffee to Go

We didn't like losing one of our own.

So she would not like that I was winging this job.

My plan was not usual.

It was not how agents worked.

I knew that.

My plan was really out there.

As far from what we do as it could get.

I would do things as far from the book as possible.

I was taking a chance.

And I didn't think the agency would like that.

Not after we just lost a man.

She could hear it in my voice.

She knew I was hiding something.

Knew I was up to something.

Something she would not like.

"What's going on, Pete?" she asked.

"Look," I said. "I have an idea."

She sighed heavily.

"I don't like the sound of this."

"I know," I said. "But you didn't give me enough time."

"We couldn't help that," she said.

"I get that," I said. "But I still want this to go well."

"What does that mean?" she asked.

"I can't do this by the book."

"Why not?" she asked.

"Because I'll end up like that kid."

Chapter 13

I heard her take in a deep breath.

I heard her let it out slowly.

"Look. These are *very* tough guys," I said. "And they weren't born yesterday."

"I know that, Pete."

"If I do things by the book, they'll know I'm an agent."

She stayed quiet.

I tried to explain.

"I'll blow my cover if I do things your

way."

She remained silent.

"I need to do this my way," I said.

"You are taking a big risk," she said.

"I know that."

"Are you sure it will work?" she asked.

"I can never be sure of anything," I said.

"I know," she said.

She sounded scared.

"These guys," she said. "They're ruthless."

"I know."

"They don't play by any rules," she added.

"I know that too."

"You can't predict what they'll do."

I had to smile.

"They won't be able to predict what *I* do, either."

She laughed at that.

"How ugly is this going to get?" she

asked.

"As ugly as I have to make it," I replied.

But I was grinning.

"Okay," she said. "So clue me in."

"On what?" I asked.

"On why you need the C-130 transport."

My grin remained in place.

"I'm bringing my lunch truck."

Total silence.

"What?!" she asked. "For real?"

"It's the only thing I could come up with," I said.

"That's your big plan?!" she croaked.

"It was the only thing I could come up with."

"There must be *something* else you can do, Pete," she said.

"Nope," I said. "I thought it through. From every angle. I just wasn't given enough time."

"So you're going to bring your lunch

truck," she said.

"That's right."

"Are you *crazy*?!" she asked.

"Crazy like a fox," I answered.

Chapter 14

The C-130 arrived on time.

I had the lunch truck ready to go.

I had cases of food and soda, too.

I'd buy the ice up in Vermont.

But I brought just about everything else.

If I were going to pull this off, I needed a full truck.

We loaded the truck onto the plane.

Then we loaded the cases of food.

"Is this it, sir?" a soldier asked me.

"That's it," I said.

The soldier smiled.

He looked at the lunch truck.

"Sure wish we had one of these while I was in Iraq," he said.

"I'll bet," I said.

"Not many roach coaches in Iraq."

I smiled.

"I would think not."

I saw him eyeing the box labeled "sweet snacks."

"Want a Ding Dong?" I asked.

His face lit up.

"I'd *love* a Ding Dong, sir!"

"What's a Ding Dong?" another soldier asked.

"Like a Ring Ding," a third soldier replied.

"What's a Ring Ding?" the second soldier asked.

"I think they call them King Dons now."

Coffee to Go

"What's a King Don?" the second soldier asked.

"What were you? Raised under a rock?" another soldier asked the second soldier.

"Sorry for not knowing what a Ring Ding, a Ding Dong or a King Don is!" the second soldier huffed.

I had to laugh.

"You sound like that Geico ringtone," I said.

As one, the three soldiers sang, "Ring-ady-ding-ding-dinga-dong. Ring-addy-dong-ding-dong."

Then they all cracked up.

I reached into the box and took out Ding Dongs for all.

I pointed to the guy who'd never had one.

"You go first," I said.

He tore off the wrapper.

"They look like hockey pucks," he said.

"Yeah, but they taste better," soldier number three said.

"And they don't break your teeth when they come flying at you," I said.

The kid took a bite.

"Hey, these are great!" he said.

I smiled.

"Yet another happy customer," I said.

I gave each of them some more.

"How much do we owe you, sir?"

"They're on me," I said. "My way of saying thanks for the lift."

Chapter 15

We got to Vermont.
We backed the truck out of the plane.
The soldiers helped me with my stuff.
For now, I packed the boxes in the truck.
All but one box.
I threw *that* box at the second soldier.
"Here," I said. "Take the whole case."
It was the case of sweet snacks.
"Gee, thanks, sir!" he said.
"And don't forget to share," I called to

him.

I didn't need to say that.

All the guys were tearing the box open.

It was like a free for all!

I had to laugh.

I drove to the bed and breakfast.

On the way, I stopped at a grocery store.

I bought lots of sweet snacks.

And ice.

Lots and lots of ice.

There wasn't much in the little town.

But I found a motel.

It was built in the fifties.

If you wanted to be nice, you'd call it "retro."

If you wanted to honest, you'd call it old and worn out.

I just called it home.

At least for the next few days.

I checked out the town.

Not much going on.

Coffee to Go

I drove by the bed and breakfast.

It looked quiet.

No cars in the driveway.

That meant I beat the weapons dealers.

That was a plus.

I could watch them as they arrived.

See who was there.

Get some recon going.

The only problem was that the town wasn't used to having a lunch truck.

So I had to get out there.

Get people used to seeing me.

I had to make it seem as if I'd *always* been there.

At least enough so I could fool the arms dealers.

Chapter 16

It's hard to change Vermonters.

They were a stubborn sort.

"But we don't *need* a lunch truck," a logger said.

"It will save you a trip to town," I said.

"I *like* driving to town!" he said.

"Okay," I said. "So drive to town, too."

He looked at me like I was an idiot.

"Now what good is having *both*?!" he said.

Coffee to Go

"You don't have to *buy* anything from me," I said.

He shot me a look.

"I'm just doing a new route," I said. "Testing it out. Seeing if it works."

"Well I can tell you right now, it doesn't work," he said.

I would have laughed at how stubborn the man was being.

But I couldn't make him angry.

I had to get accepted by this town. And I had to do it quickly.

The arms dealers were coming.

Already, one car was in the driveway of the bed and breakfast.

It was a Porsche. Top of the line.

It most likely belonged to the man who was running the auction. The seller.

I was running out of time.

I needed to be a "local" as soon as I could.

These stubborn people were going to get me killed!

If they knew that, they would help me, I'm sure.

But they couldn't know what I was up to.

If they *did*, I'd be killed for sure!

If there was one thing I learned about these people... they were honest!

So honest that they were not very good actors.

I'd have to be the one to do the acting, *if* I was going to survive this mission.

And I was starting to think that it was a big if!

I was beginning to worry.

Chapter 17

The weapons buyers came to Vermont.

They swarmed in like locusts.

Locusts who drove *very* nice cars.

It seemed to be as I'd thought.

Only weapons buyers were guests of the inn.

So it was a good thing I made the choice I'd made.

I never would have gotten in.

Not with only a few days to get known as

an arms dealer.

It just wasn't enough time.

So my plan was the best option.

It still was not a great plan.

But it was the only plan I had.

My only option.

I had to go in through the back door. So to speak.

I had to make my move.

I'd been watching things for 72 hours.

Three days.

Things were slow at first. But last night there was lots of action.

A lot of guys came in overnight.

That meant the auction was today.

Arms dealers didn't hang out much.

Too much chance they'd get caught.

So they swooped in.

Bought their illegal weapons.

Then slid out.

Like the snakes they were.

Coffee to Go

I had to move.

I couldn't wait.

I had to get in the inn.

I drove my lunch truck up to the back door.

I went into the inn.

I was in the kitchen.

A woman was there.

She was baking.

I couldn't tell what she was making.

It could have been bread. Or pasta. Or a dessert.

"Hello," I said.

She jumped in fright.

"Oh," she said. "You scared me."

"I'm sorry. I just wanted to see if your guests needed anything."

She looked nervous.

Very nervous.

So. She knew who her guests were.

Knew what they were doing.

Her face turned white.

"Are you here for..." She didn't know how to finish her sentence.

She tried again.

"Are you the..."

Once again, she couldn't finish her thought.

I knew what she wanted to know.

She wanted to know if I was there to arrest the men at her inn.

She wanted to know if I was the police.

I couldn't let her know that I knew anything.

It would put her in danger.

It would put *me* in danger, too.

It was best to act as if I knew nothing.

"I drive a lunch truck," I said.

I didn't want her to say any more.

If one of the men heard her, she'd be killed.

Chapter 18

She'd already shown that something was up at the inn.

She'd already given too much away.

The arms dealers would not like that.

They would kill her in an instant.

Just to shut her up.

She'd meant nothing to them.

And by tomorrow, they'd be gone.

So no one could track them. Or trace them to her.

They had all signed in under false names.

There was nothing saying that they were there.

Nothing proving that they were there.

Except for me.

I could prove it.

So I had to get in there.

I had to see their faces.

I had to see who was here.

They might not know *me*, but I knew them.

Over the years I'd studied thousands of files.

Seen thousands of pictures.

I'm sure I could ID all of them.

It was my job to do that.

It was my job to report who was here. And what was sold.

And who bought it.

I'd already reported the seller.

He would be arrested before he left

Coffee to Go

Vermont.

Poor guy.

He won't know what hit him!

There were seven other countries waiting to get their hands on him.

Seven!

And they all wanted a piece of him.

He'd been a ba-a-a-a-d boy.

Made quite a few enemies.

And now that we had him? We didn't mind sharing.

This slime bucket would not see the light of day ever again.

I'm sure we'd send him to the country that wanted him most.

The country in which he'd done the most harm.

They'd get first crack at him.

And if he survived their prison system?

He'd go to the next country that wanted him.

Chapter 19

That would be his life for the rest of his days.

Not fun.

But we wanted the buyers, too.

So that's where I came in.

"I do my own baking," the inn-keeper said.

"That's nice. But your guests might want something now," I said.

She tried to stop me.

Coffee to Go

I was glad of that.

The men would see that she tried to keep me out.

That was good.

It would keep her safe.

"Hey, guys," I said. "I've got my truck out back. Anyone want a snack?"

They all sat there in shock.

"I've got pizza, cake, chips, coffee, sandwiches. If you're a health nut? I've got yogurt, granola, fruit."

"Who is this guy?!" a man asked.

His voice had a heavy accent.

He was from the Middle East.

I knew who he was right away.

We'd been looking for him.

He was on a *few* lists.

He had his hands in quite a few things.

"I drive the lunch truck here in town," I said. "Need a jolt of caffeine? I make a *great* cup of coffee."

The arms seller yelled at the woman behind me.

"I *told* you no one was to come in here!"

She looked terrified.

Before she could reply, I spoke.

"She didn't know I was coming," I said. "She bakes for her guests. She'd never *invite* me."

Then I laughed.

I tried to get everyone to relax.

But the tension was high.

It could not have been just because of me.

Something must have gone wrong before I got there.

This was an angry crowd.

The sale was not going as planned.

"***Leave!***" the seller shouted at me.

Then he turned to the inn-keeper.

"***You too!***" the seller shouted.

"Okay," I said. "Chill out. I'm gone."

Chapter 20

I didn't leave all the way, though.

I left through the back door. Then I rolled to the side of the screen door.

I heard the woman in the kitchen.

She let out a gasp.

I knew what was coming.

I took my gun from my boot.

I swung open the screen door.

I shot the seller. Right before he tried to shoot the inn-keeper.

The problem was, his gun had a silencer on it. Mine did not.

I knew the buyers would come in shortly.

Guns blazing.

I grabbed the woman.

I shoved my keys in her hand.

"Take the lunch truck," I told her. "Get out of here. Do not come back until I call you. There is a cell phone in the glove box. I will call you on that phone."

"B-B-But..." she stammered.

"Go! Stay away! I will call you when it is safe to come back. Now *go!*"

As she was leaving, a blaze of bullets sprayed through the kitchen.

Great. Automatic weapons.

I slammed the door behind her.

Then I dove behind the stove.

Good thing she hadn't turned it on yet.

I would have been badly burned.

But she really should pre-heat.

Coffee to Go

I'd have to tell her that when I called her.

A hail of bullets came flying at me.

All of the arms dealers pushed through the kitchen door. They were all shooting at me.

"You don't want to do this," I called to them.

The bullets kept flying.

I had a mirror in my wallet.

I took it out.

I edged it past the stove.

I saw where they were all standing.

Then I started to shoot.

I picked them off. One by one.

They went down like dominoes.

Starting with the guys on the right.

You'd think the guys to their left would have the sense to run. But no. They didn't.

By the time I got out from behind the stove, I was the only one alive.

"Great," I muttered to myself. "Now I'm going to have to do a *lot* of paperwork."

We hope you liked the second book of...

PETE'S PLACE

NOX PRESS
books for that extra kick to give you more power
www.NoxPress.com

Want comedies?

Try reading...

THE SMITH BROTHERS

NOX PRESS
books for that extra kick to give you more power
www.NoxPress.com

Everyone has it
within them
to be a

LEADER

Do **you**?

NOX PRESS

books for that extra kick to give you more power
www.NoxPress.com

The

LEADER

series.

HONOR
COURAGE
RESPECT
SERVICE
INTEGRITY
COMMITMENT
LOYALTY
DUTY

(We bet you can't read just one!)

And if you haven't
read them yet,
you might want to
check out...

Junkyard Dan

(A series of comedic crime dramas.)

NOX PRESS
books for that extra kick to give you more power
www.NoxPress.com

We also have...

the very funny

A LEEG OF HIS OWN

series.

NOX PRESS
books for that extra kick to give you more power
www.NoxPress.com

Want to read more NOX PRESS books?

Go online to
www.NoxPress.com
to see what's being released!

Books can easily be purchased online or you can contact **Nox Press** via the Website for quantity discounts.

Are you a fan?
Do you want us to put *your* comments up on our Website?
If so, please e-mail them to:
NoxPress@gmail.com

NOX PRESS
books for that extra kick to give you more power
www.NoxPress.com